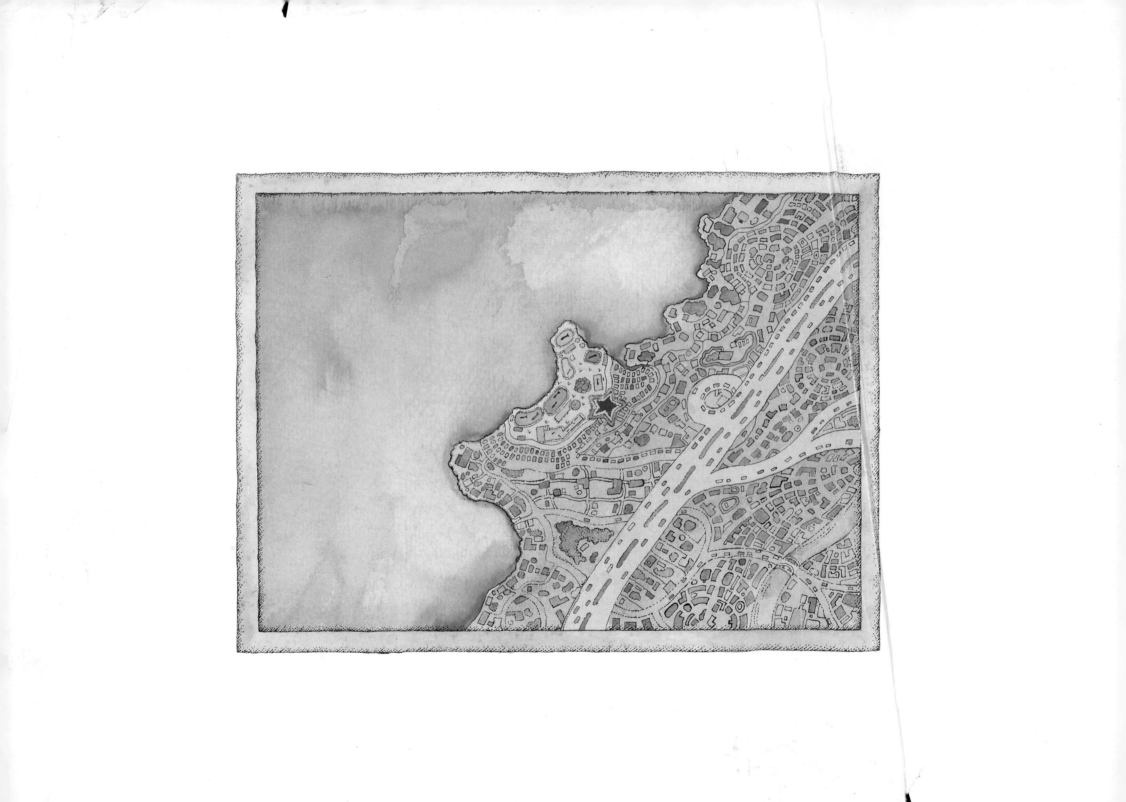

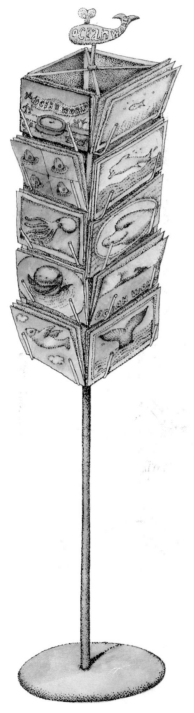

Peter Sis

AN OCEAN WORLD

Greenwillow Books, New York

'92

Library of Congress Cataloging-in-Publication Data
Sis, Peter.
An ocean world.
Summary: A whale sails new seas and, after several
unsuccessful attempts, makes a friend.
ISBN 0-688-09067-2. ISBN 0-688-09068-0 (lib. bdg.)
[1. Whales—Fiction. 2. Stories without words]
I. Title   PZ7.S6219Oc   1992   [E]—dc20   89-11692   CIP   AC

unp

To all who care about our world

Greetings from Ocean World!
This morning I saw a whale
who has been here since she
was just a few weeks old.
Soon the day will come when
she will be returned to the ocean
to live with others of her kind.
She has seen many people but has
never seen another whale. I wonder
what it will be like for her!

Love
Peter

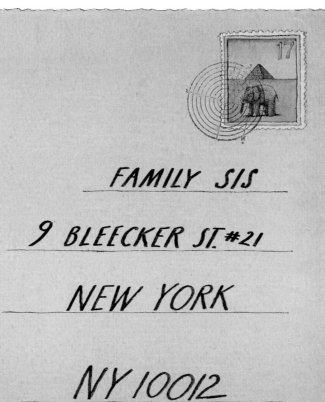

FAMILY SIS

9 BLEECKER ST. #21

NEW YORK

NY 10012

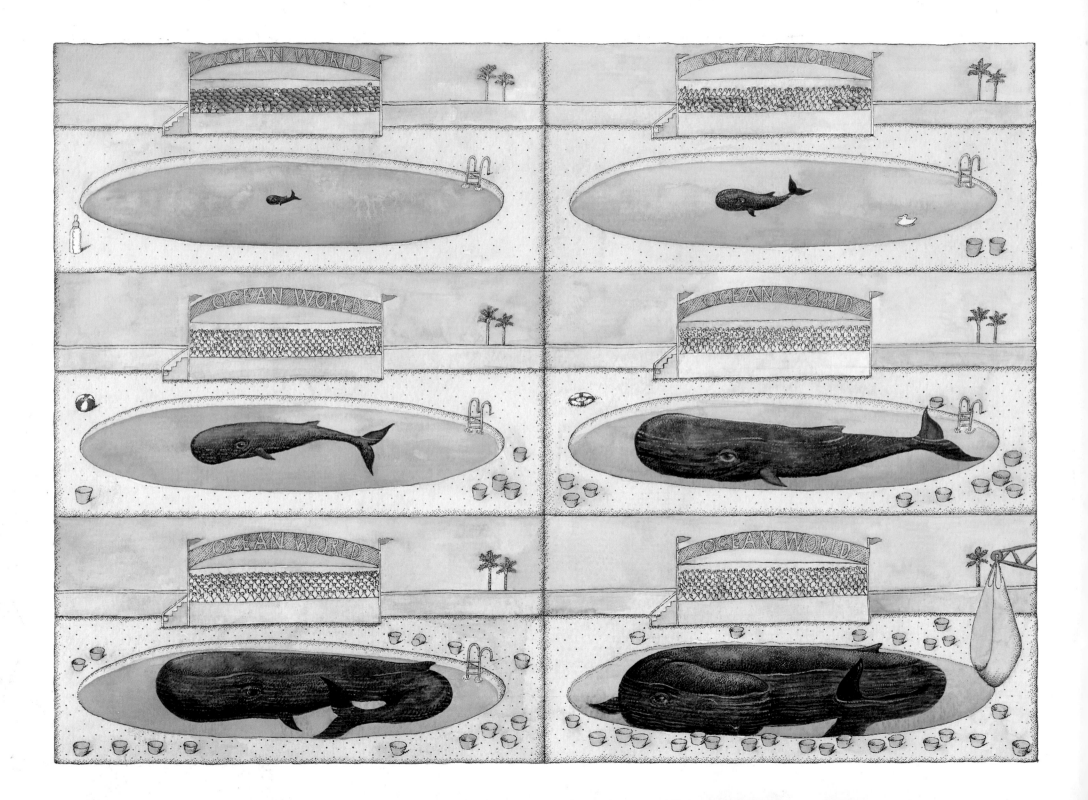

The whale grew

and

grew

and

grew

until…

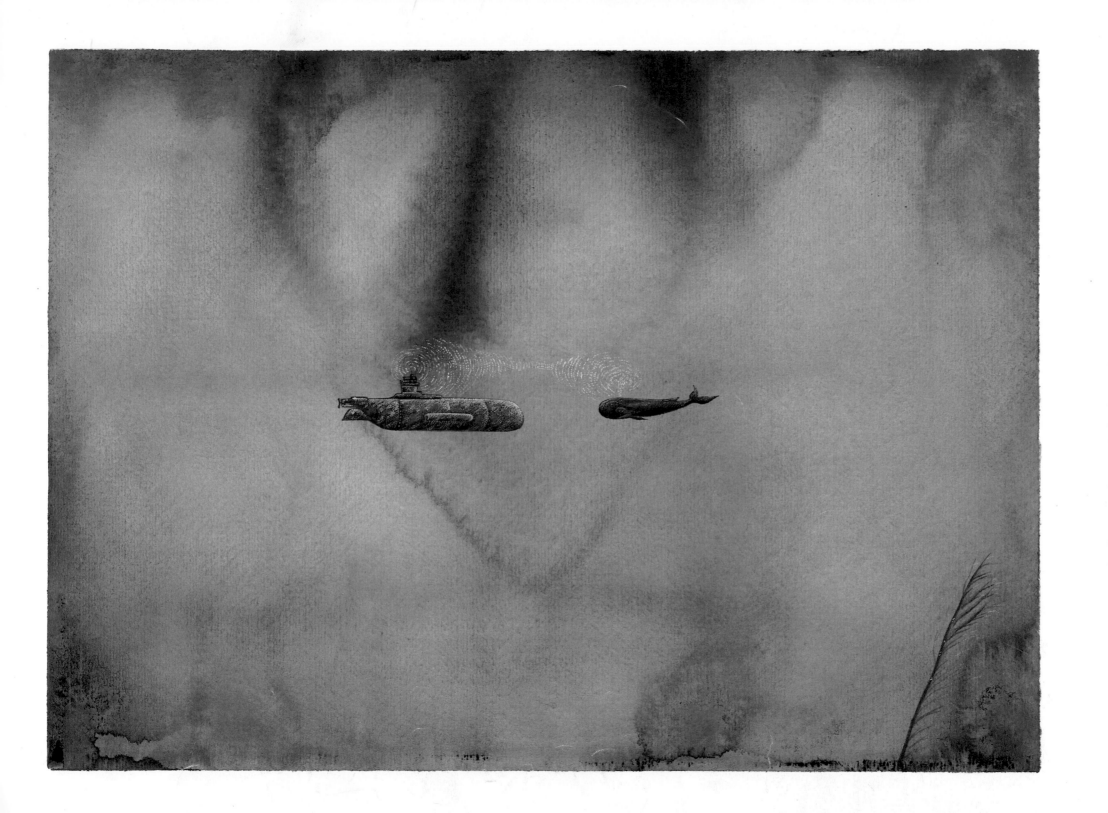

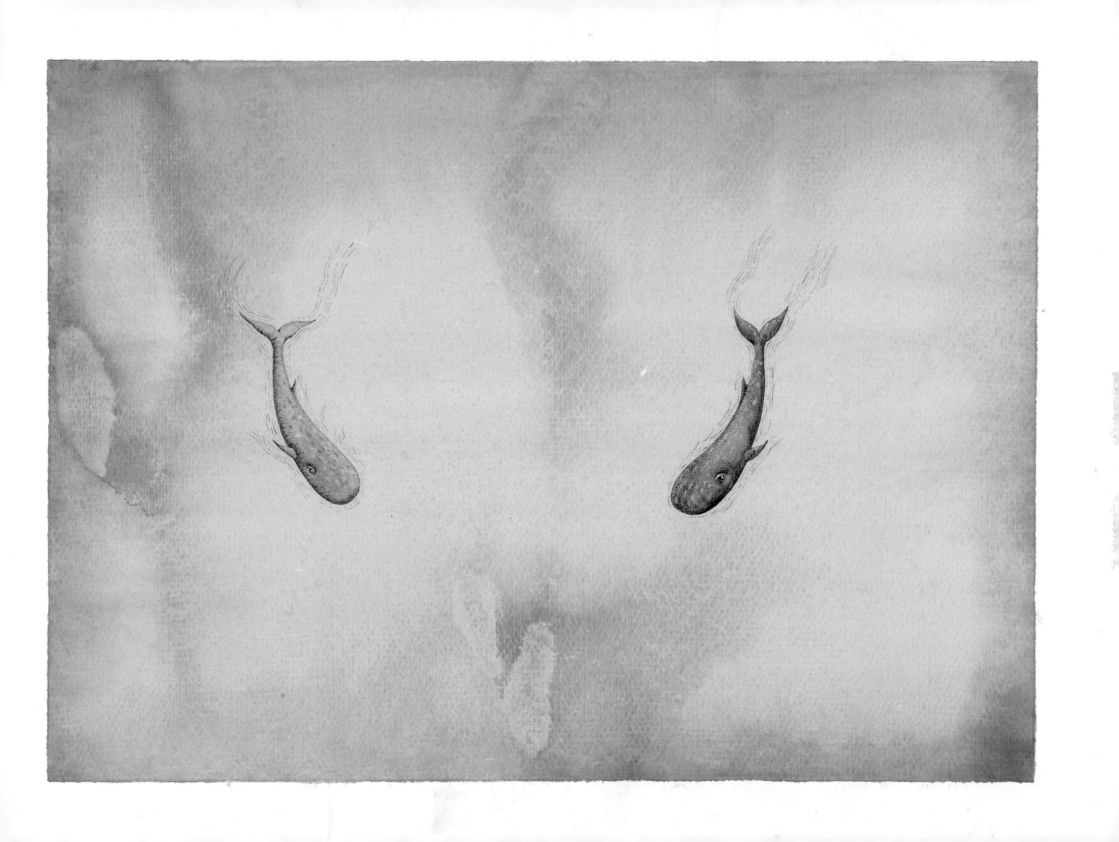